Put Beginning Readers on the Right Track with
ALL ABOARD READING™

The All Aboard Reading series is especially designed for beginning readers. Written by noted authors and illustrated in full color, these are books that children really want to read—books to excite their imagination, expand their interests, make them laugh, and support their feelings. With fiction and nonfiction stories that are high interest and curriculum-related, All Aboard Reading books offer something for every young reader. And with four different reading levels, the All Aboard Reading series lets you choose which books are most appropriate for your children and their growing abilities.

Picture Readers
Picture Readers have super-simple texts, with many nouns appearing as rebus pictures. At the end of each book are 24 flash cards—on one side is a rebus picture; on the other side is the written-out word.

Station Stop 1
Station Stop 1 books are best for children who have just begun to read. Simple words and big type make these early reading experiences more comfortable. Picture clues help children to figure out the words on the page. Lots of repetition throughout the text helps children to predict the next word or phrase—an essential step in developing word recognition.

Station Stop 2
Station Stop 2 books are written specifically for children who are reading with help. Short sentences make it easier for early readers to understand what they are reading. Simple plots and simple dialogue help children with reading comprehension.

Station Stop 3
Station Stop 3 books are perfect for children who are reading alone. With longer text and harder words, these books appeal to children who have mastered basic reading skills. More complex stories captivate children who are ready for more challenging books.

In addition to All Aboard Reading books, look for All Aboard Math Readers™ (fiction stories that teach math concepts children are learning in school) and All Aboard Science Readers™ (nonfiction books that explore the most fascinating science topics in age-appropriate language).

All Aboard for happy reading!

An All Aboard Reading™

Station Stop 1

Collection

Girls Will Be Girls

Grosset & Dunlap

**The All Aboard Station Stop 1 Collection:
GIRLS WILL BE GIRLS published in 2003.**

Published by Grosset & Dunlap, a division of Penguin Young Readers Group, 345 Hudson Street, New York, NY, 10014. ALL ABOARD READING and GROSSET & DUNLAP are trademarks of Penguin Group (USA) Inc. Published simultaneously in Canada. Printed in the U.S.A.

ISBN 0-448-43334-6   B C D E F G H I J

An All Aboard Reading™ Collection · Station Stop 1

Girls Will Be Girls

By Maryann Cocca-Leffler, Joan Holub,
Wendy Cheyette Lewison, and Jane O'Connor

Illustrated by Maryann Cocca-Leffler, DyAnne DiSalvo,
Julie Durrell, and Jerry Smath

Grosset & Dunlap
New York

Table of Contents

Nina, Nina BALLERINA

By Jane O'Connor
Illustrated by DyAnne DiSalvo

Nina wants to be
a ballerina.

Every week

she goes to dance class.

She can stand on one leg.

But not like Sara can.

She can do a split.

But not like
Sara can.

Sara is the best in the class.

Soon there will be
a big dance show.
Nina's class will be butterflies.

Miss Dawn picks Sara
to be the queen butterfly.
Nina does not mind.
Not too much.

That night
Nina tells her mom,
"We all get wings
and bug masks.
Sara is lucky.
She is the queen.
She gets a crown.
Sara's mom will know
it's her right away.
But the rest of us
look the same . . .
How will you know it's me?"

Nina's mom gives her a hug.
"Do not worry.
I will know it's you."
But Nina is not so sure.

The next week the kids try on
their wings and masks.
"You are lucky,"
Nina tells Beth.
"Your mom will know you
because you are so tall."

Then Miss Dawn claps.
The class is ready to start.

"Pretend you have wings,"
Miss Dawn tells the class.
"Pretend you are flitting
from flower to flower."

Nina does just what
Miss Dawn says.
She tries hard to be
a good butterfly.

Nina goes over the steps
to the dance
all day . . .

. . . and all night.

It is the day
before the dance show.
Nina is in the park.

"Watch me flit
from flower to flower,"
Nina says to her friends.

Nina leaps.

She feels like she has wings.

She feels like a butterfly

even if she is not the queen.

"Watch out!" her friends yell.

But it is too late.

Nina falls.

Nina's mom takes her
to the doctor.

Nina's arm is broken!

The doctor puts a cast on it.

The cast is so heavy.
Nina does not feel like
she has wings anymore.
Nina starts to cry.
"It will stop hurting soon,"
her mom says.
Nina sniffs.
"That is not
why I am crying.
I can't be
in the dance show now!"

But Nina's mom
calls Miss Dawn.

"Miss Dawn says
you can still be in the dance.
You will be a butterfly
with a broken wing."

That does not sound
so hot to Nina.
But she does not want
to miss the dance.

It is the next day.

The show is about to start.

Nina's tummy feels like
it is full of butterflies.

The music begins.
"Just do your best,"
Miss Dawn tells the class.

That is just what Nina does.

Can Nina's mom
tell which butterfly
is Nina?

She sure can!

Nina, Nina STAR BALLERINA

By Jane O'Connor
Illustrated by DyAnne DiSalvo

Dance class is over.
Nina runs out to Mom.

"Hooray!" Nina shouts.
"There is going
to be a dance show.
Our dance is called
Night Sky."

Mom and Nina drive home.

"Eric is the moon,"
Nina tells Mom.

"The rest of us are stars.
We twinkle around him."

That night
Mom and Nina look
at pictures in the album.

There is Nina the butterfly
and Nina the elf.
"Soon we can put in
new pictures,"
says Mom.
"Pictures of my little star."

The next day at lunch
Nina sits next to Ann.
Nina likes Ann best
of all the girls.
She tells Ann
about the dance show.
"I am a star," Nina says.

"That is so great!"
says Ann.
Then she pokes
Beth and Emily.

"Guess what?" says Ann.

"Nina is in a dance show.

And she is the star!"

"Cool!" says Beth.

"Wow!" says Emily.

"The star!

You must be so good."

Nina does not know
what to say.
She is <u>a</u> star.
She is not <u>the</u> star.
But all the fuss is nice.
So Nina eats her hot dog.
She does not say a thing.

At the next dance class
Nina watches Miss Dawn.

"Point your hands.

Point your feet.

Be pointy like a star,"

Miss Dawn tells the girls.

"Then spin and twinkle

around Eric

the moon."

Nina learns
all the steps.

But sometimes
her feet will not do
what she wants.
And spinning is hard.

"Better,"
says Miss Dawn.

But Miss Dawn
never says "Great"
like she says
to some kids.

Nina is glad
Ann cannot see her.

On Saturday
Ann comes over to play.
They hide out in a cave.

The cave is made of sheets.

It is cold in the cave.

But they must hide

from the bear.

"Grandma called,"
Mom tells Nina.
"She can't come
to the dance show."

Ann looks at Nina.
"Nina, could I come?
I would love
to see you dance."

"NO!" thinks Nina.

"Yes," says Mom.

"Of course you may come."

Now what will Nina do?

That night
Nina cannot sleep.
The show is in three days!
Ann will find out
Nina is not a real star.
Maybe Ann will not like her
anymore.

The next day
Nina has a plan.
It is not a good plan.
But it is the only plan
she can think of.
All day she limps
around the house.

She limps in the supermarket
and at the pizza place.
"My leg hurts,"
Nina keeps saying.
Nina does not look at Mom
when she says this.
She does not like to fib.

That night Nina takes a bath.

"My leg still hurts,"

she says.

"Maybe I can't be

in the dance show!"

Mom looks at Nina.

"Do you <u>want</u> to be in it?"

"Yes!" says Nina.

But then she starts to cry.

Nina tells Mom everything.

Mom tells Nina to tell Ann.

"Ann will understand,"

says Mom.

Nina is not so sure.

At school Nina sees Ann.
"Ann, I have something
to tell you.
I am not <u>the</u> star of the show.
Three other kids are stars too.
It is no big deal."

Ann shrugs.

"So what?

I just want to see you dance."

Then she gives Nina a locket.

It looks like a star.

"I hope you like this.

It shines in the dark."

It is the day
of the dance show.
Mom and Ann are there.

Up goes the curtain.
Nina is a star—
a pretty good star.

67

And she is the only one
who <u>really</u> shines.

Nina, Nina, and the COPYCAT BALLERINA

By Jane O'Connor

Illustrated by DyAnne DiSalvo

This is Nina.

And this is Nina, too.

She is new at dance class.

Miss Dawn says,

"I will call you Nina 1 and Nina 2."

Nina 2 is a good dancer.

And she is nice.

She helps Nina 1 with her splits.

After class,
she always shares
her candy bar.

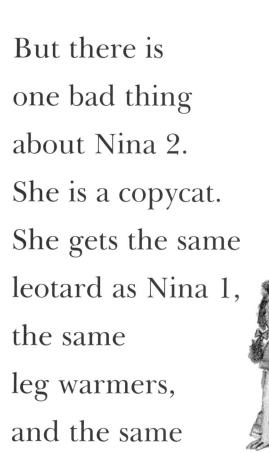

But there is
one bad thing
about Nina 2.
She is a copycat.
She gets the same
leotard as Nina 1,
the same
leg warmers,
and the same
dance bag
with a key chain.

"Look!" Nina 2 says one day.

She takes off her hat.

"My hair is like yours!"

says Nina 2.

"Now we can be like twins."

Nina 1 does not say anything.

She does not want

to be like twins.

She wants to be just herself—

Nina.

That day Miss Dawn
tells the class about
the next dance show.
"Each of you will make up
your very own dance."

Nina is excited.

In the car she tells her mom,

"We have to think up

all the steps.

The dance can be a solo.

That means you do it

by yourself.

Or it can be a duet—

that means you do it

with another kid."

At home Nina thinks
about her dance.
Yes! She has a cool idea.
She finds an old wand.

She tapes on ribbons.

She will do a solo.

She will be a rainbow!

At the next class,

Jody and Ann work on a duet.

They are puppets on strings.

Eric is doing a solo.

He is a karate guy.

He does kicks and twirls

and a back flip!

Nina works on her dance.

She runs and leaps.

Then she runs and leaps

some more.

"Very nice," says Miss Dawn.
"But try to put more steps
in your dance."

In the dressing room,
Nina 2 comes up to her.
"I'm not sure
what my dance will be.
Maybe I will be a rainbow, too."

All of a sudden Nina gets mad.

Very mad.

"No!" she says.

"That's <u>my</u> idea.

And you can't copy it."

Nina 2's face gets all red.

Nina 1 gets her dance bag

and walks away.

All week Nina tries to make
her dance better.
She does not think
about the other Nina.
She sees herself
in the mirror.
She tries twirls.
No good.

She tries splits. No good.

She ends up poking herself
in the tummy.
It does not hurt that much.
But Nina starts to cry.

"My dance is dumb,"
she says to her mom.
Then she cries harder.
She tells Mom about Nina 2.
"I feel bad. I was mean.
But she is such a copycat."
Mom understands.
"Tell her that you're sorry.
But also tell her how you feel."
Nina wants to.
But that is hard . . .
even harder than doing
a good split.

She waits for Nina 2
at dance class.
"I am sorry I yelled,"
she says. "I <u>like</u> you.
It's just—"

Nina 2 stops her.

"It's okay. I am sorry, too.

I will stop being a big copycat."

They both laugh.

Nina 2 smiles.

"Too bad I can't do

a dance about a copycat."

Later in class
Nina 2 comes up to Nina 1.
She has an idea for a dance—
a duet.
Nina 1 thinks
the idea is great.

It will be cooler than her
dumb rainbow dance.
So they talk to Miss Dawn.

They spend the day together.
Nina 1 has good ideas
for the costumes.

Nina 2 has good ideas
for the dance steps.

They work hard together.
They have fun together, too.

At last it is the day of the show.
Nina 1 and Nina 2 do their duet.
Nina 1 is a black cat.
Nina 2 is the same black cat
in a mirror.

They pounce.

They prance.

They paw at each other.

At the end
everybody claps and claps.
Sometimes it is fun
to be a copycat!

Pajama Party

By Joan Holub
Illustrated by Julie Durrell

Tonight is my pajama party.

I can hardly wait.

My friends are coming over.

And we plan to stay up late.

Ding-dong! Look who's here!
It's Meg and Jen and Dee.
Keesha's here, and Emma, too.
That makes six, with me.

Mmmm . . . .

The pizza's ready now.

Quick! Let's go and eat!

After that, banana splits
make a yummy treat.

The sky is black.

The moon is bright.

And all the stars are out.

It's party time—let's boogie!

We sing! We dance! We shout!

No one wants to go to bed.

Let's stay up all night instead!

We paint our nails with polish—
all sparkly blue and green.

Then we fix each other's hair.

Jen looks like a queen.

Dee passes out some bubble gum.

Then she blows a bubble.

We can't believe how big it is!

Uh-oh. Bubble trouble.

No one wants to go to bed.

Let's stay up all night instead.

Emma starts a pillow fight.

We whack and whomp each other.

Pillows zoom across the room.

Oops! I got my mother!

We munch on chips and popcorn,
while a movie plays.

Then we get our bedrolls out
and put on our pj's.

But no one wants to go to bed.
Let's stay up all night instead.

Emma gets the hiccups.

Keesha gets the wiggles.

Jen, Meg, and Dee tell jokes.

And me? I get the giggles!

Next we all share secrets
and tell ghost stories, too.

I put on a big white sheet.
Look out! I'm coming! <u>Boo</u>!

Now we snuggle in our bedrolls
and hug our pillows tight.

We must not close our eyes because
we <u>must</u> stay up all night!

But Keesha yawns

and stretches out.

Dee doesn't make a peep.

Meg and Emma rub their eyes.

And Jen falls fast asleep.

Everybody's snoozing now.
Everyone but me.
I'm not sleepy—not at all.
It's only half past three.

I close my eyes a minute,
just to take a break.
It may look like I'm sleeping,
but . . .

. . . I'm not—I'm wide awake!

PRINCESS
FOR A DAY

By Maryann Cocca-Leffler

Last week Jessie went to
the moon in her spaceship.

Yesterday Jessie
climbed a mountain.

And she camped in the woods.

Today she is a princess.

She has a crown to prove it.

And tomorrow there will be
a Royal Ball.
She makes invitations.

Come to a
Royal Ball!
It will be at 9:30
in the morning.
Wear your best
gown.

She gives the invitations
to all her loyal subjects.

Later Princess Jessica
gets the royal garden
ready for the ball.

Then she finds
a ball gown.
She puts gold bows
on her shoes.

The next morning
Princess Jessica comes downstairs.
She has on all the royal jewels.

"Jessie, why are you wearing
a curtain?"
asks her sister Kelly.
"My dear sister,
I am Princess Jessica.
And this is my ball gown,"
says Princess Jessica.
Kelly rolls her eyes.

"Queen Mother,"
says Princess Jessica.
"What will we have to eat
at the Royal Ball?"
"Will milk and muffins do?"
Mom asks.
Princess Jessica nods.
"The Royal Ball must end
at 12 o'clock," says Mom.
"Uncle Steve is taking you
out to lunch."

Soon the Royal Ball begins.

All the loyal subjects
wear their best gowns.
They sip milk
from pretty teacups.

They dance and sing.

They even ride
the royal horse.

At noon Princess Jessica
waves good-bye to everyone.

Princess Jessica runs
into the house.
It was the best ball ever!

Just then Uncle Steve arrives.

"I found this on the front steps,"
he says.

"I think it belongs to
Princess Jessica," says Mom.

"So this is Princess Jessica!"
says Uncle Steve.
"Well, let's see if the shoe fits."

"It fits! It fits!"

shouts Princess Jessica.

"My prince has come!"

Uncle Steve bows.
"Now we will go
for a royal pizza," he says.
Princess Jessica takes his hand.
"Jessie, you can't go out
like that!" Kelly calls
after her.

"Of course not!" says Mom.

"You forgot your crown!"

Princess Buttercup

A Flower Princess Story

By Wendy Cheyette Lewison
Illustrated by Jerry Smath

160

In the magic garden,
six Flower Princesses
open their eyes.
Wake up, wake up!
It is the first day of spring!

There is going to be a party.
Princess Lily and Princess Tulip
set the table.

Princess Rose gets
the band ready.

Princess Hyacinth makes a cake.

Princess Iris plays ball.

She does not like to work.

She likes to play.

But where is Princess Buttercup?

Princess Buttercup is
out picking buttercups.
One buttercup here.
Two buttercups there.
Now she has lots of buttercups
for the party.

Look!

It is a butterfly.

"How pretty!" she says.

She follows the butterfly.

She forgets all about
the buttercups.

She forgets all about the party.

The butterfly hops
from flower to flower.

Princess Buttercup skips after it.

She looks around.
Where is the butterfly?
And where is she?

Oh, no!

She is in the woods.

And she is lost.

But the butterfly is not lost.

It is still looking for flowers.

Princess Buttercup has an idea.

She holds up a buttercup.

Then she sings this song:

Butterfly, butterfly,
Bright as can be.
Fly, pretty butterfly,
Fly down to me!

Soon the butterfly sees
the buttercup.
Down, down it flies.

Now the butterfly is just
over her head.

She grabs hold of it and . . .

Whee!

Off they go!

At last,
there is the magic garden.
Princess Buttercup is not
lost anymore.

182

Down, down comes
Princess Buttercup
on the butterfly.

183

Plop! The butterfly lands
on a flower.

Princess Buttercup
climbs down.

The Flower Princesses are
happy to see her.
And she is happy to see them.

The party begins.
Everybody has fun.

Even the butterfly!

KATE SKATES

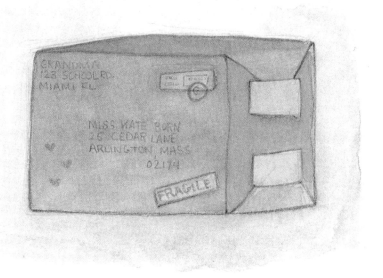

By Jane O'Connor
Illustrated by DyAnne DiSalvo

I am so happy today.

I just got new skates.

They are for big kids.

They have only one blade.

Grandma sent them

for my birthday.

My sister is happy, too.
She is happy because
she has my old skates.

Grandma also sent a little skirt.
Now I look like
the skaters on TV.
"Let's go," I tell my little sister.
"Let's try our skates."

Now my little sister
does not look so happy.
"I do not know how to skate,"
Jen says.
But I tell her not to worry.

I will show Jen
how to skate.
That is what
big sisters are for.
Mom takes us to the rink.
"Oh, look!" I say.
"Diana Lin is coming here."
I have seen Diana Lin
on TV lots of times.
I want to skate like her
someday.

My little sister and I
put on our skates.
It does not take Jen long.
It takes me longer.

"I am coming, Jen,"
I tell her.
"Do not be scared.
I will hold your hand.
I will help you . . ."

But my little sister
does not need help.
"This is fun,"
she says.
"Come on, Kate."

I walk to the rail.

My skates look so cool.

My skirt looks so cool.

I can't wait to skate.

Right away
I find out something.
My new skates
are harder
than my old skates—
much harder.
I slip.
I wobble.
A big kid crashes
into me.

There is only one thing
I am good at—
falling!
I fall lots of times.

I do not look at all
like the skaters on TV.
I see a big kid laughing.
I am glad when it is time
to go.

A week later,
we go back to the rink.
I try skating again.
And do you know what?
I am not as bad
as the last time.

I am worse!

"Hold my hand.

I will help you,"

Jen tells me.

She is being nice.

But <u>she</u> is the little sister.

<u>I</u> am the big sister.

I do not want her help.

All of a sudden, it gets noisy.

Diana Lin

will skate soon.

Great!

Now everybody

has to get off the ice.

Great again!

I am sick of skating.

But Jen wants to go around

one more time.

Jen skates away.
She is out pretty far.
She does not see
a big kid coming.
Oh, no!
He is going to crash
into her.

"Jen! Watch out!" I yell.

I wobble out to help her.

That is what big sisters are for.

I pull her out of the way.

But now I cannot stop.

I spin around and around
like a top.

Then I crash into somebody.

Down I go!

"Here. Let me help you."

I look up.

It is a pretty girl

in a pretty dress.

I have seen her on TV

lots of times.

It is Diana Lin!

Diana Lin smiles.

"That was some spin!"

But I shake my head.

"It was not on purpose.

I can't skate."

"I bet you just need some help.
After my show,
I can help you.
Deal?"

Is she kidding?
Me and Diana Lin!
"Deal!" I say.

I watch Diana Lin.
She can jump . . .

and spin
on purpose.
Wow!
Is she good!

Then Diana Lin

comes over to me.

She holds out her hands.

I am scared.

Everybody is looking.

What if they laugh

like that big kid?

But I take her hands.

She shows me
how to push and glide.
It is like Diana Lin is
<u>my</u> big sister.
Around the rink we go.
Push, push, glide.

And do you know what?

I am not as bad as before.

I get better!

I even let go of her hands
for a little.

I am skating on big-kid skates!

That night,
Diana Lin is on the TV news.
And do you know what?
So am I!

Maybe I will be as good
as Diana Lin . . .
someday!